Sarcasm, Humour, Love and Twist.

Unstable Relationship

Subhransu Sekhar

Published by Walnut Publication

#172, K8, Kalinga Nagar

Bhubaneswar - 751003, India

www.walnutpublication.com

ISBN: 9788193843680

First Published in July 2019

Dedicated to all the Confused Lovers.

Acknowledgement

I had no idea why a person who was perfectly stable before, quits his or her job and joins the author's community, even realising that he or she will be earning a little penny. But after writing and discovering the true feelings of an author, I have received my answer, that why there is a unique feeling of being an author. Friendship is one of the hardest things to explain because a true one inspires and a bogus one degrades thinking capability. I would give well-deserved credit to Mr. Abhishek Behera, debut author of Pulitzer At 16, the one who inspired me to discover my potential to complete UNSTABLE RELATIONSHIP, and gave his unbiased suggestions which helped me to complete my book.

Never the less, completion of the book was never possible without the blessings and support of my parents Mr. Muralidhar Sahoo and Mrs. Suchitra Sahoo. I would also mention my uncle, Mr. Debasis Sahoo, who came across my manuscript and gave his special efforts to complete the publishing process.

I would give a huge thanking note to "Tusar" from Walnut Publication, the publishing consultant who made the publishing procedure much simpler than I had thought it to be and made my queries solved.

Overview

"Love is not complicated, but the right love has a different spark from others."

UNSTABLE RELATIONSHIP is a self-descriptive fictional account of Adarsh Rai who has expressed his life-story in the form of words. His thoughts about life and his love-life are being expressed with some humour and a few unexpected twists. From his childhood to his adulthood, all the positive, as well as all negative experiences, are being described with the expected series of events and some unexpected chain of turns.

The unique part of UNSTABLE RELATIONSHIP is that every chapter of the book begins with a self-composed poem about the unconventional ideas of life. The seven chapters consist of love, struggles, chaos, and humour combined and being presented by the protagonist cum narrator himself.

Introduction

"I was busy wandering at the majestic yet lovely house. The house was extraordinarily beautiful, and the walls of the house were decorated with oozing luxury. Starting from the grand velvet sofas to the majestic chandelier, every corner of the house was perfectly decorated with stunning pieces of luxury and ultra-modern furnishing. Suddenly my eyes fell on a wall neatly decorated with a string of photo frames. As I approached further, I was stunned to see a picture which was in close resemblance to that of Alia. But honestly, I didn't know that something was awaiting me that would give the greatest shock of my life, something of which I had never expected something..."

"My heart beats lower downed to 40s, and my heart got an ache, and my kidneys got a stroke, whereas my brain was factory reset. These all happened by realizing the meaning of the statement stated by Alia..."

Join the journey of Adarsh as he explores his love life in a way which is packed with an expected series of events and unexpected twists and turns. Adarsh love story isn't just about love but also an account of some unconventional thoughts and truths on which we often turn a blind eye. His journey might be somewhat similar to you, but I'm sure his unexpected series of twists and turns is something I consider to be rocket science. Join me in discovering some of Adarsh's love events which are full of chilling events and humorous love accounts, which made him, say his relationship status as UNSTABLE RELATIONSHIP.

Contents

1. **CHAPTER ONE**
   Boyhood in Primary School 2
2. **CHAPTER TWO**
   Teenage at A New School 12
3. **CHAPTER THREE**
   Discovery of Potentiality 24
4. **CHAPTER FOUR**
   Lessons of Life 33
5. **CHAPTER FIVE**
   Descending the Stairs 42
6. **CHAPTER SIX**
   House No. 99 52
7. **CHAPTER SEVEN**
   Uncovering Thoughts 63

World Within You

People will criticise all and ever;
Even you are right or wrong,
They will never stop.

But you should never stop;
On chasing your dreams ever,
Because this is your life; not others.

You have to stop running with others,
And be the king of the world.
You have to be separated and survive alone.

The dream is your, not others.
You have to discover;
The world within you, not others.

CHAPTER ONE

Boyhood in Primary School

Born in a middle-class family, I was silent, a socialised fellow who loved discovering new things on any field; except studies. I had a typical 2000s old school childhood and felt the effects of nostalgia often about the childhood memories that I miss these days. Influenced by my family members, I too got triggered to acquire a job in banking in the upcoming future. In childhood, when I was a student in my school; I regretted for the enjoyment I could have done the last year that I didn't do. As every child wishes, I also wished that I could become an adult as soon as possible so that I could do things that were restricted during childhood. I remember how my mother used to force me to take a short nap during the afternoons, which have become heaven during these busy scheduled days.

I changed my school in 9th grade as my father had a transfer in his job (which created a major impact later on). Studying in one school since the last ten years and transferring into a new school with new rules and regulations gave me immense loneliness at the initial days. I got a lack of interest in studies which made me fail in my 9th-grade finals. The loneliness was not the only reason for failing in physics examination, but there was a case of an affair of the heart. Failing in the finals and getting a compartment was very disappointing at a new school, new class and in front of new classmates. This dragged me into a massive depression, where I first time experienced and learnt the meaning of depression.

I remember when an unexpected miracle happened. A senior from 12th grade, changed my life, turning an average student to 89% in 10th-grade final examination. I remember his name, Kavesh. He not only inspired me but also supplied sample papers and golden tips that helped me to make my game. He was a very fun-loving guy, and at the beginning, it was a very awkward movement for me to accept him as a helping guide.

One day, he found me alone; sitting in the school library, thinking about future and doubting if I could be promoted to 10th grade. I was sitting with a reference book issued from the library with some random chapters opened, where eyes concentrated somewhere else other than the book. Out of nowhere, he came from the senior side classroom, and he asked me why I was sitting alone, without any friends, silenced and with a typical sad soul face with some teardrops on the face. I willingly told everything about failing an exam to secure the minimum marks to pass, alone in front of other new classmates in a new school and how disappointed I was from this. It was very difficult for me to express thoughts to me that I had a decent standard in studies, and was one of the front benchers. He smiled and just told me, 'one never fails, either he wins, or he learns'. He then narrated some experiences that how he failed to keep 40% in the 10th grade and at that time he achieved the second rank among all the state high schools. It was very hard to believe him because the way he talked and walked, with a cunning smile on his face gave me the first impression of the image of a person who had sweetness on his lips and venom in his heart, and to whom no one would ever believe him. But gradually, I realised that judging a book from its cover page is a foolish decision as listening to him, created a positive bond between us and I trusted his advice and moved on in life. Preparations started from zero levels for the compartment exam that was to be appeared by me for the only one subject that was physics. With the remaining days of gap for the exam, I tried my level best and finally got promoted to the 10th grade.

I blindly followed him and his advice without doubt, and I thank my past, for listening to his angelic advice without any ego. In this selfish world, I found an angel who selflessly helped me out. Coming to 10th grade, I got addicted to motivational books. I had no intention to read to the whole book but read only the acknowledgement part, the contents and the back-cover page where some of the gist of the book was being written. Gradually, 10th grade became the class full of unconventional memories and became the best class with memories of school life. The whole year when I was in my 10th grade, I missed Kavesh Bhai (brother). The three months of deep priceless relationship with him were some of the best moments of my second school. He passed out of the school after appearing in the 12th-grade exam.

Ending up 10th grade with a lot of memories, and some new experiences became the best year of my school life. But my life was not as simple as it looked. Talking positively is the best way to start any conversation, but you know, the most common quote and inspiring quote, - "Life is not a bed of Roses." What my life looked till 10th grade, was not as simple as it looked.

I remember when I was in the 1st grade; I was a very shy and innocent boy who was very quite in the classroom. I rarely talked in the classroom. At the lower classes, our school used to make seat children on one bench, one boy and one girl to make children quite. My seat was also changed, and I sat with a girl named Velina. At those days, that was very awkward even if we were only eight years of age. We became good friends, and we sat with each other for two consecutive years. Then at 3rd grade, we sat separately, but the connection of friendship remained constant.

The bond between us became strong, and everything went well. We used to share jokes, talked about the secrets and had good conversation daily. We used to take our best characters from the cartoon series and mimicry their voice and actions. The feeling of friendship became deeper, and at last, something happened that proved again wrong the fact, "that a boy and girl can never be a best friend forever."

During my 6th grade, I fell in love with Velina, from her innocence and the way of expressing things to her caring nature. I was too young to love anyone as seen in typical Indian culture, but it just happened. We all know that the first love has some different energy and a unique feeling that I also got. Coming to 6th grade, everything changed slowly. I don't know how, but the whole classroom got a small clue about my secret crush. My classmates used to tease me with her name, where I could never stop myself from blushing.

Through the confidence and courage which I gained from one of her best friends, I proposed her in 7th grade, although by not telling her directly, but through a love letter from taking tips from Bollywood movies. That was one of the most embracing things that I did during my initial teenage days. On the day of giving the letter, I was very much excited and also curious to hear her answer. I remember, I wrote, *"I don't know you love me or not, but I love you a lot."* That was written by a short-heighted boy who acted to be mature enough, literally me at the age of 13 years old. That was my first experience of expressing my love with the magic of words (laughs).

Giving that piece of paper made me so nervous that by giving it to her hand, I ran away from her. A certain scare revolved around me as doing such things made me think about the consequences that would have happened if she would have discussed it with her parents. Some part of my heart was excited for her to reply. Seeing some of the young couples from my grade, I had already imagined my situation after getting a positive reply. From standing under a secret shed in the school to presenting chocolates and sharing the same with each other. But unexpectedly, her answer was 'No'.

I tried my best to catch-hold of her attention and tried hard enough. When it comes to the case of a girl to a teenage boy, he can do wonders or blunders to impress or depress her. At the 8th grade, I planned again to propose her, with full preparations as if I was going to crack a competitive examination. But before that, some of the couples from our school were caught red-handed by the principal of our school. Due to this, a lot of controversies were created. Parents of the couples who were being caught were called due to which a lot of dramas and chaos were being created. I don't know how but Velina knew all about the plans that I made to propose her and she one day asked me to leave all these sorts of plans and also leave her. She reminded me that I was too young to be involved in this love chaos. It brought an ego within me, and after that day, we never talked again. This was my first experience of love, and I learnt how destructive and constructive love can be.

There was nothing good between us. But then I was admitted into a new school by the end of the 8th grade. A new phase of life started, and I had no idea what was waiting for me.

Keep Moving On

Life is a walk; keep walking,

With struggles and difficulties incoming.

Life changes with a blink of an eye;

People forget you saying goodbye.

People you love, you cannot express;

Haters always make you depress.

People will insult you with blame;

They will do the best for decreasing your fame.

If the cause is the truth, no need to worry;
Without any fault, no need to say sorry.

Keep moving without any hesitation;

Because there is a limitless destination.

CHAPTER TWO

Teenage at A New School

As usual, I started going to the school regularly considering myself slowly as one of the members of the gang who were controlling the whole classroom. Coming to a new school with all new classmates, new teachers and new situations, made me think about the past fun, I used to have before. Sometimes I got some of the flashbacks of Velina, and some of the vintage jokes in that old school. The experiences were totally different from the past old school. In the mean time, I tried to train myself of not falling in love once again, considering the new school, but I was wrong; because you know *'Dil hai ki Manta Nahi'* (this silly heart doesn't listen to you). I was in my teenage, and here falling in love was going to cost my carrier in taking one wrong decision.

Days passed and months too. Then I slowly got adjusted with new classmates and remembered each and everyone's name. Facing new classmates, talking to them directly was very difficult for a boy who was very shy and had no known friends. It was never comfortable sitting with some unknown friends and trusting them.

One day our class got an arrangement period which was a leisure period for us. The arranged teacher who came to our class seemed very modern, unlike the other teachers. I was new to the school, so I didn't know much about the teacher. Our class was a mischievous class and kept shouting aloud. The arranged teacher knew some of the students of our class as she was one of the old staffs of the school, unlike me. She asked one of my classmate girls to sing a Bollywood song. She was well acquainted with the students, and she knew well that students loved Bollywood songs and through listening the music, sung by one of the classmates will make them bound to remain silent for a certain period of time.

Then a short-heighted girl went to the podium in the class and fearlessly sang a Bollywood song. I had no interest in listening to the song as I had pretty much assignment to complete. I just continued to complete my tasks. As I was writing in my notebook, I was introduced to a high-pitched voice that was somewhere travelling from the front of the class to my ears. The vocalist was a unique combination of sweetness and crispness, which forced me to look upwards keeping the assignments aside. I discovered her name as Parul. Her voice was so melodious and sweet that within some seconds, the class became pin-drop silence. The teacher's mind game worked!

From the beginning of the track, one boy was closely observing the girl, with rapt attention till the end of it and didn't even miss a single part of it. He was non-other than me. I was literally stunned seeing such a talent present in our section. Singing so well in front of all her classmates without a bit of shyness, was not a small task. While she was returning to her seat, she walked as if as was the only queen of my dreams.

Since that day, I created different excuses to talk with her. Sometimes I asked her class notes to write; sometimes, I took her stationery pouch to play with it and sometimes slowly pulled her hair so that she could chase me in order to beat me. I fell in love again. That's how it all started to love with Parul, one of the students with great grades of our class. (The beginning of a cute love story?)

Life begins again with new hope, new energy, and new school with a new love. All the precious and special time I spent with Parul, made me distracted from studies as days passed and unfortunately karma did its work and gave me a compartmental in science examination in the final term (although she kept on topping in studies). I regretted not studying at the right time and lost hope of everything. Thanks to God, who came in the form of the senior brother who helped me out as I mentioned before. This was a believe created by me as we Indians always believe in these beliefs. I followed him, his advice, his way of thinking and analysing and his way of planning. He opened my eyes, inspired me and helped for creating the best possible version of me.

Promoted to 10th grade, it was one of the main years for the students. I was well-settled and aimed high for the year. Everything was going well, and the year brought many experiences of life that were unforgettable. I believe that this year had those experiences which made the best year of school life. Parul and I got closer and became good friends.

Things started to change when I started to work. It was very difficult at the beginning studying something that I failed. I hated physics, so I started with it. Initially, opening the physics book; understanding the sums and practicing my own seemed as if I was an ant was trying to climb the Mount Everest.

After ending up a controversial 9th grade, I made some of the new friends gradually. Avesh was one of my classmates with whom I ended up with a strong bond. It all happened through a small incident. He loved to pinch people very hard in order get some fun as he loved the reaction of the students and one day, I had to bear that pain as I was not excluded from it. Continuously I got pinched, but I didn't react anytime and always took that as fun. One day, he pinched me hard on my shoulders, the position, were the last night, I took tetanus. I reacted very hardly and unconsciously as I slapped him hardly one his cheeks. The fair skin guy got his cheeks red.

But as soon as I slapped him, I regretted my action and asked him to forgive me. He had a very good impression with all the teachers, and I got scared of what would happen if he complains my name to the teachers. I was a new student, and I was sure that the new school was not going to leave me if Avesh complains about this to the class teacher. But he forgave me without any terms and conditions. That day was a nightmare for me as I regretted of my action for some initial days. An invisible bond was created among us gradually, and we became good friends and bench partners. We cracked jokes and practiced together physics problems. Life became good, and my marks improved.

In the meantime, I told some of my friends about Parul, and that was one of the biggest mistakes that I committed. Again, everything got ruined when one of my closest friends told everything to Parul. Luckily, she didn't overreact to this and talked as she was talking before. She just ignored the fact and enjoyed her life as always. As the final boards approached nearer, we became unconsciously serious in our studies and often talked less in social media due to family pressure to do well in the board results. One day she literally blocked me on her all social media accounts, and she texted me "I hate you." I got a breakdown by her message as everything was good, and there were no issues between us.

Later I tried my best to talk with her, but she had no interest. After putting so much effort to talk with her, she finally revealed that one her friends who stayed nearby her house, revealed everything about me to Parul's parents, but she managed her parents and settling the matter. She was very much annoyed with me and didn't want me to talk to her.

The 10th-grade final examinations were very near, and hardly there was less than a week to exams to be started, and all these sorts of things happened. This dragged me to despondency.

In India, all parents, teachers and relatives are result oriented only, and they don't care about anything else. All they need is good marks in academics. This is how I was also targeted. Surrounded by such despondency, and pressure of fetching good marks in exams, created a certain situation that was impossible to describe through words for me, but I had no other choice. Basically, in the native language, there was a proverb- "wound on a unseeable place can neither be seen nor shown to others" which suited me right.

But I had the only option left with me that to read and fight with the situation so that to stay not out on the crease.

I remember, while the preparing holidays were given for the boards, the time when I was preparing for the exams, unconsciously teardrops made wet my notebook. Nostalgic feelings always won over the conscious mind. It was very difficult to learn and remember facts about a chapter because I don't know how suddenly the memories with Parul struck in my mind. The same tears came while I was writing in the answer-sheet in the examination hall. I knew how difficult those times were.

Basically, it is really a minor step to move on from such situations, but most of us fail to take that small step to move on. We often take such situations lightly and make fun of the person who is suffering from such disaster but putting on the same situation can help us know how it feels. It wasn't easy to survive until and unless you are playing with the feelings.

Now the declaration of results was nearer. I had no idea about the results. As the days of declaration of results came nearer, the number of times running towards the temple increased. But I had to accept the fact that what I had written was going to be evaluated but not the aftermath situation. Unfortunately, that was the time when the messages like- "Share this message to ten people or you will fail in your exams" went on viral on social media. If we don't share such messages, an uncertain fear approached in the conscious mind which was unbearable. We were forced to share such messages due to the fear of exams. But deep inside, we all know that was of no use.

On the day of results, when I checked the website, I felt as if I was the most underrated successful man who was present on the earth. Somehow, I managed to get 89% in 10th grade, but achieving that percentage at such critical situation was one of the greatest achievements for me. I was very happy with my results, but my parents expected more, as usual. This is India, where marks matter more than talent.

Life Is A Walk

The life you are living is a walk;
Neither morning; nor evening.
People leave you with aggression;
But never stop your progression.

You will wish to take revenge;
You will wish to do the damage.
But stop that thinking process;
And rebuilt yourself and progress.

Life is a walk; that you have to walk.
Never downstairs; rather upstairs.
Stop thinking about people who left you alone;
As one day, you are going to stand all alone.

Never take revenge from someone;

As you have to become better from everyone.

People regret when you are above them;

As you progress day by day without them.

CHAPTER THREE

Discovery of Potentiality

The most difficult part of school life arrived when I got into 11th grade. But the feelings I had for Parul never reduced. Again, coming to 11th grade brought massive changes, bringing new classmates and new subjects. Life went on as usual. Coming to the new class, Parul's misconception and frustration she had against me of reduced as the normal talks began again. Our classes and streams changed as I opted for commerce and she opted for science, but the same old me had turned into a lost wanderer, searching for the love that I had never seen.

Looking a right day and right time, I proposed Parul on her birthday. Guess what; I was rejected again. And this time, her decision was right. She loved someone else who she never revealed before. She had a mindset that a clear rejection was better than creating a fake promise. This was the strange aspect of being in a relationship; some bold actions taken at the right time can save your day in a lot many ways. She never wanted to ditch someone, and I respected her decision, but it was very hard on my part to accept it. She wanted a stable relationship, and according to her judgement, I was unstable. Now, to be honest, this word was almost like a setback for me, I was lost in the search for the true meaning of that reply. It was a kind of thing I never expected. I accepted everything but being called as unstable shattered me and trust me, it was hard enough on my part to regain the so-called self-confidence & self-belief that I believed to have lost long ago.

Accepting my weakness, I moved on. Although those sleepless nights with red eyes and tears never stopped for several months, I pretended that nothing happened to me. This incident compelled me to force my laughter and fake my smiles because I believe humans are double-faced creatures. I pretended to be normal as usual, but I only knew what I was undergoing with. Tears had turned into frozen crystals that were nothing more than mere droplets, but those droplets spoke volumes about the feelings that I was burdening my heart with. I showed everyone that I was strong enough and rejection had no effect on me, but every time I tried to reflect these artificial emotions, I knew I was wrong.

Being heartbroken and wounded from inside, I decided to work on self-improvement so that I can move on, leaving my past behind. As I said before "moving on is one of the most difficult tasks". I attended various self-improvement seminars, worked on a number of odd things and read some motivational and self-improvements books, but these were only materialistic recreation. Some of them worked, and the path of improvement began. I was fortunate that I took commerce and had time to work on the shattered aspects of my life. The experiences are what I needed because "experienced people are more mature than merely aged people."

The maturity within me improved when I got someone to work on my life. Well described in the words of a Commerce student, I formed some kind of a joint venture with him. I saw the dawn of my life with that guy. He was Rajesh. We both were bench partners in the 11th grade. The mindset of both of us matched as we had gone through the same situation.

(Not love. Laughs.) He was a type of person who was crazy for the airlines as well as politics, whereas I was interested in technology. It was a unique combination of friendship which turned into a brotherhood. We cracked jokes that we both only understood. We went to different concerts and loved talking about topics that were logically illogical to my other friends. Life started to be good again. In the meantime, my family had to shift our house to another locality. The house where we got shifted was in a colony. The colony was a very new experience for me as of before we were living in a rented house.

Later on, I discovered that he was an author; but the best part of him was his down to earth personality. I had no interest in writing, but when I read the book "The Illogical Author", written by Rajesh Saxena (my bench mate)

I realised about writing that anyone could write, but everyone cannot express. A writer is not a person who writes well; a writer is the one who can express an ordinary thing in an extraordinary way. This was the only book which I read completely, as all the other books I have read were only the main points and some highlights that were mentioned in the back-cover page as I mentioned before.

Ending up 11th grade was the only intention for me, and I did it with a good margin. But now, the most important, the 12th grade arrived – the last grade, where school life ends. The 12th grade started with new hope. The main aim was to score a good percentile which was considered to be a golden ticket to a reputed college. I had decided to focus on 12th grade. I thought that I would participate in each and every competition to keep some wonderful memories. The year started with joy, which didn't last long. Students were scribbling notes and were putting endless efforts to achieve something called "good marks."

This year had a lot of pressure on me as well as the teachers as well as on the school itself. The school in which I enrolled myself in the 9th grade taught me a lot of new experiences and left me with a lot of memories. The time eventually came of which every single family member and so-called relative was waiting for. The final 12th-grade boards arrived. This was the last exam for school life, and earlier I had never kept 90%. That was a wish, and this exam was the best opportunity to get one.

I worked hard this time, unlike the 10th-grade depression; the word "unstable" was my motivation. Keeping all distractions aside, I made it a point that I won't let any kind of distraction to just barge into my mind like earlier.

The exams went well, and the hope of getting 90% eventually increased. For the first time in my life, I got something that I expected. I got 91% in my finals. That day was not that joyful until the felicitation day came. The day of felicitation was the best for my parents as well as for me. This was the first time ever, where I was rewarded for the studies other than any extracurricular activities. This was the thing that I missed in 10th grade. Like this the school life ended with unlimited experiences and numerous memory. The nostalgia of school life kept reminding me of both the schools in which I had read. One had the memories of Velina and one with the memories of Parul. Now it was the college life which was going to start. I had a good percentage in the 12th grade, so I had a good opportunity to get myself enrolled in a good college.

The word 'unstable' was the only reason for which it compelled me to put the real efforts and show the real potential within me. I discovered that the person who works hard should never fail. Even if the consequences become worst, and the situation asks you that you have lost it completely; but your self-confidence will never let anyone defeat you.

I had no idea about what new chaos was waiting in college life. With the experiences earned until date, I learnt that all the bad experiences were building me whereas all the good experiences were motivating me to work. This helped me either to get satisfied with what I was doing or else improve what was lacking. This was a type of positive approach. There is also a famous saying that- "A person who can stay positive in a negative situation always wins." This quote was the reason which compelled me to stay positive in negative situations as well.

Ask Me

When life backfires you and asks you;

"You have lost it", but I still stand by you.

Ask me how it feels,

When People ignore and mess with you;

Ask me how it feels.

When people demotivate and hate you;

Ask me how it feels.

When you are dragged into controversies;

Ask me how it feels.

When you have to stay not out on crease;

Ask me how it feels.

When people talk rubbish behind you;

Ask me how it feels.

When they break you psychologically;

Ask me how it feels.

CHAPTER FOUR

Lessons of Life

Finally, I got admitted to a college near my colony. In the initial days, I went to the college with the college bus in which some of the co-passengers were my colony members. In college life, the scenario with school life was completely different. Here I found that students had no interest in studies, and they only believed in merry-making. Making friends was very easy with other college mates for only those who had good exposure in school life before. A lot of schools lacked the facility of giving the right exposure to the students. But I was lucky as the situation was different for me. Being a commerce student, the level of pressure of studies was less in comparison to a science student. But the friend circle around me was not as good as I had in school. I had controlled my best of not getting influenced by any of the bad companies till the end of school life, but unconsciously, I slowly got involved in activities that the society thought was illogical and was not expected by a student who belongs to a family with some decency. I got addicted to smoking and drinking, failed in each and every examination of the semesters and almost flunked the first and second year of college life.

In the meantime, the private company under which my father was working since last two decades, was going to remove my father from the job as the company was lacking sales and they were forced to remove employees in order to do some cost-cutting. There was a situation in my family where some of them ignored the situation and some limited people in the family supported us. The company gave a limited one year of time for searching a new job. Even the time period was enough for us, but my father was in his 50s, due to which there was a lot of difficulties for him to find a new job out. Here even the experience failed. We, the nuclear family started searching jobs online and offline as well.

I remember how it all started. One day while returning from college to home, a group of some senior college mates surrounded me in front of the college gate and a situation of ragging was created. They all started to create a one versus all situation because they thought that I was different from them and their ideas of college life and my ideas in college life were colliding in the same arena. Due to that, they recorded my video of being scared and the face of fear that was created because recalling the past life I had not faced any of those situations before. That day I felt like I left my balls at home. Since that day, I became a new entertainment for them. I did things what they wanted me to do. This was not because I feared of coming across that situation again, but due to the fear of that video which was recorded by them would be leaked. They knew that mental harassment was much more powerful than physical harassment. And unconsciously after being used by them for their entertainment, I was given an offer to join them. I don't know why, but I accepted their proposal. This was in order to get rid of the situation. But I had no idea that I would have become one of the chain smokers in the next few months. And that is how it all started. I forgot my passion and goals of being an entrepreneur and continued living as if a lost loser. That was the point where I realised how difficult it is to quit smoking or drinking for a person if he or she once gets addicted to it, knowingly or unknowingly.

On one cold evening, I along with my other fellows Madhu and Prayash were standing in front of a betel shop in a lonely dim-lighted road and were smoking a cigarette on hand and checking social media with the Smartphone on the other. We were criticising the Indian political leaders as if we're standing in the elections. I saw a random popup advertisement on my Smartphone. It was about a coaching class advertisement and where 95% was highlighted broadly. I laughed at the advertisement as seeing the broadly highlighted 90% on it. They both were also eager to know the reason as I showed them the advertisement critiquing the market strategy to invite the students into a trap. I asked them randomly that was there any future plans for them as we had already lost our first year in the college.

Madhu replied" Kya bhai? (What brother?) Why so tensed? What plans? I have nothing to do. After completing all that more three to four years of studies, I will continue my father's business and settle. My life is set as usual."

I asked Prayash about his planning for the future as well.

"My father is handing a well-reputed hotel. Similar to Madhu, after completing all my basic studies, I will handle my father's hotel", Prayash replied.

Listening to Madhu and Prayash, my motivation for smoking and enjoying the ongoing life broke into pieces that were impossible to rejoin again. My mind literally went blank as I had never before. A thought came into my mind that, what about me? What would I do? Putting the cigarette down, I went home, asking both that "I have an unfinished urgent work to do." This was the most common dialogue to get rid of friends according to me.

After reaching home, random thoughts approached within my mind. Neither my father had a proper job, nor did he have a proper business so that I could manage it after my studies. He had less than 6 months, within which he had to search for a new job and join a new company. He also didn't have that much sum of money, so that he could start his own business so that I could handle it in the future.

I saw my future's dark side until and unless I took action. I thought that who will help me out? That Madhu or that Prayash ? Will I become a driver for Madhu for earning or become a waiter in Prayash's hotel to feed my family. A state of depression approached me, where I was surrounded by thousands of thoughts.

I kept silence and remained at home for a week, thinking about where I started and where I had come. What I was before two years and what I have become in the last two years and how I got influenced by bad company and became a chain smoker.

A thought strokes my mind- "I was a good student means above average, and now I am not able to pass in the examinations. I remember before I wanted to be an entrepreneur and earn good sums of money so that the struggle my family has seen before will be able to settle happily."

A strong desire went inside me that what I have already done can never be changed. But I can do move on with the aim to do something. I was the only child in the home, and I was the one who had to do something to make my family survive. I thought of doing something extraordinary do backup all that wasted times and all.

Game of Life

We live in a life;

It hurts when you are alive.

The game of life is hard to play;

But those who play it; they live happily.

Men and women will come;

And of course, you will definitely come.

But you have to wait until that;

Because you have to hustle till that.

Your day will surely come;

You will shine all alone.

Because you will be happy one day;

As you have hustled every day.

All those sleepless-nights will pay off;

Dollars and Euros will come up.

When your hard work pays off;

Keep walking in life; every day up.

CHAPTER FIVE

Descending the Stairs

Our college was at the end of the session and there was to be our annual function conducted in our college. I was interested in trying something new, but I had no intention to sing or dance. Then, only one option was left with me, and that was to become a volunteer. So, I registered myself as a volunteer.

So, I was given the duty of the stage volunteer. I was looking after the costumes of different participants. There were numerous emotions among the participants. I observed the consequence that some of them were nervous, while some of them were excited, and some were biting their nails. As I was busy observing the participants, my eyes fell on something that took my attention for a while. My eyes fell on someone who was descending from the stairs in a hurry. The bright spotlight almost covered her face. I don't know why, but I started getting butterflies in my stomach, the moment I saw her descending from the stairs.

After a matter of seconds, I was introduced to a beautiful display of a girl whose looks were no less than an incredible mixture of beauty and innocence.

She was searching for someone in despair, looking mostly more than just confused. I was still struck with her beauty; I was unable to remove my eyes from her face. After searching here and there in despair, she ended up crashing near me with her confused look. When she approached me, she started talking in the top of her voice, which was somewhat a frustration as the work she wanted was not done. The moment she landed near me, I started getting shivers down my nerves, my legs trembling, my heartbeats almost skipping a beat and my throat was almost at the stage of drought. Her argument was that no one was present at the backstage to look after the participants, and there was a total mess back there, and she wanted someone to handle this messy backstage crew. Rather than listening to what she was telling I was struck with her looks.

I still remember her face with was a perfect blend of cuteness and soft innocence with her glowing eyes. Her hair was fluffy, and it was a perfect match for her incredible looks on her face. In my view, she was a living fairy, as if her face was something that didn't belong to the human race. She was wearing a traditional white saree, and her curvy figure gave it the right fit. To me, she was something that I had never seen before.

She was one of the anchors in the annual function, and her bright eyes made me dumb in front of her. I tried to observe actions and the style of anchoring at the backstage and a situation came when we both had a massive eye contact from far enough. I got a sense of love at first sight, and I was curious enough to know more about her. I rapid fired several questions at that same night of the annual function during a small interval. But unfortunately, this round of rapid-fire questions made her more nervous as she was being questioned by an unknown fellow. Due to this, she just got her devil side and her anger dominated over me. I felt ashamed as I was given duty in the stage, and I was doing all these irrational things. In the meanwhile, the function ended well, and everything went right. I thought I had no life as the girl whom I liked at first sight; I made her angry by putting some irrational questions to her.

On the same night when I reached home, I regretted my actions, and I realised that how I messed things up. There was a gap of two days to college as the college had to reconstruct the environment which was messed with wires, lights and chairs due to the annual function. As usual, as I went to the college classroom, I saw a girl whose looks were no less than an incredible mixture of beauty and innocence, the same charm and the same bright eyes with some unconventional emotions was standing in front my room as if she was waiting for someone fearlessly. I wondered that "kash mere liye koi ese intezaar karta!" (if someone waited for me as she was)

Seeing me coming towards her, she waved her hand, indicating as she was talking to me. I knew that it is impossible where any girl approaches me for any conversation. I thought she was waving to someone else, and I ignored her. Then I was about to enter the classroom, where she stopped me from entering. I realised that she was the same girl whom I saw in the annual function and whom I irritated.

"Sorry, Adarsh for my behaviour in the function." She said.

Listening to my name from her mouth seemed as if I was a celebrity since ages. I got a hormonal imbalance by her appearance again, and her smartness compelled me to think she was a science student.

I replied her politely" Sorry was to be said by me as I asked you the irrational questions that made no sense during the annual function." Although I said this, my voice broke as if I was being encountered.

Then the bell rang which the most embarrassing part not because the college was about to start, but because the sweet argument was about to end. The conversation between us ended as she headed back to her classroom. I was dumbstruck that what was happening in the last ten minutes. Then unconsciously when she was leaving to her classroom, I asked her about her name.

She looked back and smiled. There was a hidden shyness in her smile, which almost melted my heart. She replied in the next step as she walked away - "Alia".

Then days started and ended with the glimpse of her face. Her smile and way her way of talking made in fall for her. Jordan was in love again.

Now it was the final year in the college. The schedule of the exam within the admit card was with our hands. This time there were no obstacles in studies as everything was going with me. This was the time where I could say- "Apna Time Aagya." (It's my time now) I prepared for the exam with full motivation as I was now prepared for my graduation.

It was the first day of the exam. And guess what, as I entered in the examination hall the look that was hanging on the faces of the poor examinees made me show some pity to them but eventually, I realised that I too was a victim like them and I was also to be tested by the educational system. But trust me, I had no idea that something was waiting for me. I saw Alia sitting in one of the benches in the classroom. I can say that this was like adding ghee in the fire. As I entered the room and checked my roll number and found the seat, I realised that it was the seat beside the seat of Alia. There were desk arrangements for two seats in one bench, and I was sitting beside to Alia. On day one, butterflies were roaming in the stomach, and now it was like I was flying along with the butterflies. Then I realised that I was the in the examination hall and not in a botanical garden. I wished that if that would have really happened in the garden.

By no time, the exam started. As I was writing all the basic information on my examination answer sheet, an unknown sweet smell approached towards my nose. I was confused about where the smell was really coming from. I smelled my answer-sheet, but there was no sign of any smell. As I rotated myself, I learnt that the smell of the fragrance was coming from Alia. This was the first sign that what I was going to write in the examination hall was uncertain. The question paper was distributed, and I was distracted seeing her milky white skin. I had no idea what I was doing was right. I completed the answers hence and forth. I had no idea that what I had written in the answer-sheet.

At the end of the examination, Alia enquired about how I did the paper. Listening that, the inner me was shouting to me that "I was looking at you the whole three hours, whereas the mind was answering the questions in the answer-sheet."

I replied that the paper was great, and I ran away from a bit of blush on my face. That's how the first day of examination started. It all ends good till the end of the remaining papers.

Unlimited Potential

A man has potential,

This helps him portable;

From one place to another,

From poorer to richer.

If charcoal can turn into a diamond;

With the passage of time.

So why one can't become a billionaire;

With the passage of time.

Develop skills through practice;

Work like a beast.

A man has unlimited potential;

He can do anything through a trial.

Keep working hard every day;

Because of success visits on a random day.

Chase your dreams and work on goal;

Else keep begging to people like a fool.

CHAPTER SIX

House No. 99

I completed my graduation. With the passage of time, Alia and I got into a good contact. We exchanged our numbers and used to go on movies and concerts as friends. I accepted her that she was the one who was perfect for me as there was a good understanding between us. I decided that she was the girl I was looking for. She was the one who could stay stable, and the dark mark on me that was set on of being unstable by Parul could be removed as Alia, and I could have got a stable relationship. I thought that- "abhi nahi toh kabhi nahi" (Now or never) I planned an idea to propose her and my gut feeling was saying that she would accept it with a "yes". The day I fixed for the same was in the month of September as I heard from her that she was shifting her home near our colony. But I had no idea that God had a different plan for me.

It was the month of August where a popular Indian festival, "Rakshyabandhan" falls. It was festive of a brother's love for his sister, where a brother promises his sister to save from all the obstacles in her life. I was happy sleeping in my home as it was a holiday for us. My mother woke me up with some postcards with her hand. There were Rakhis in the postcards which were sent by my cousin sisters from different states of India. I woke up with a happy mood and my mother tied all the Rakhis on behalf of my cousin sisters.

I saw an unknown lady who came into our house on the eve of the festival. She was holding some sweets, and from her conversation with my mother, I discovered that she was one of our new neighbours who shifted their house recently. I talked with her as she asked about how my academics were going on. It was a pretty good conversation between us. She ended up the conversation by inviting me to her home. She had a daughter who had no brother and sisters in the nearby. She wanted me to go to her home as she wished that her daughter would tie me a Rakhi. It was a very awkward movement for me as I was going to be introduced to an unknown girl whom I had to accept her as one of my sisters. I had to accept her proposal to show a kindly nature. I decided to go to her newly shifted home within the colony, which was three blocks away from our home. I asked her that I would reach there in half an hour as she gave me the block and house number.

I left to her house as promised with two Tiffin boxes and chocolate to present her as a gift. The tiffin box was full of sweets that my uncle had brought the previous day. (Laughs) In India, it is very common of exchanging sweets like soan papdi, gulab jamun and rasgulla, particularly during Diwali. (Another popular Indian festival) The sweet that any family relative brings during these festivals go on revolving around the colony and gets delivered back from where it all started. As I was going on the roads to reach the destination, I saw some stray dogs on the route. The poor stray dogs seemed hungry as I fed some biscuits that I had brought in my pocket. An unconscious feeling came to mind that how lucky I was as I was going to have a new sister where these poor stray dogs couldn't afford that luxury. I felt that I was so lucky that I was going to get Alia as my better half whereas, those poor stray dogs were so unlucky as they would never get the feeling what I got while recalling the name of Alia. I moved forward under the sheds of the green trees, birds chirping loud, and the sunrays fallings through the gaps of the tree leaves. There was a very positive vibe around the atmosphere.

Enjoying the nature on the road, seeing the small kids playing on the playground in the morning, and listening to the senior citizens' group having a talk an intense talk on the politics on the road, I reached the third block and the house number ninety-nine. I was very nervous before pressing the doorbell, as I verified the house number twice with the paper that the aunty wrote her address. As I pressed the doorbell, the door opened instantly, which gave me a shock. I saw Radhika, who was Alia's best friend. She was also pretty much shocked seeing me on the door, as aunty welcomed me to her house. I was a little bit confused and wandered that I was going to be a brother of my love's best friend, but I had no idea that another surprise was waiting for me to come. Aunty made me sit on her sofa as she went to another room along with Radhika.

I was acting discipline on her house and wandering unconventional thoughts that Radhika was the daughter of aunty, and after making Radhika as my sister, I would go closer to Alia as Radhika would help in building a strong relationship. I observed each and every furniture and electronics as my eyes fell on a photo that gave me an intense shock. The photo was of a girl who was looking at the exact copy of Alia standing along with aunty. The photo was a little bit farer from me, so I thought that it was an effect of thoughts of over thinking of Alia. (blushed) I stood up and went closer to that photo, but as I went nearer, it was clearly visible that it was a photo of Alia. As I was going deep inside the thoughts about that photo, Aunty called me from behind.

As I rotated myself towards my behind, my mind went blank. I saw Aunty along with Radhika and Alia was standing beside her holding a typical Indian brass tray which consisted diyas and sweets. It was a pleasant surprise to see Alia in Radhika's house. I thought that she might have come to enjoy a day at her bestie's house on the precious occasion, but I had no idea that what I predicted at that time, was going to be proved wrong. Aunty asked me to have a seat. Then Aunty asked to tie the rakhi, and I happily showed my hand to Radhika who was standing beside Alia. Alia came forward with the typical brass tray and tore the wrapper of rakhi. Seeing that gesture, I got impressed more as it depicted that helping nature of Alia, which compelled me to think again that Alia was going to be mine perfect life partner. But the next few seconds became my worst nightmare as Alia came nearer and tied me the Rakhi. (What?)

As she kept her fingers on my fist, to tie the rakhi, I removed my hand. All the three were confused to see my gesture. Aunty enquired about it. I replied politely that if Radhika was going to tie me rakhi, so why was Alia doing that job. Listening to Alia's name from my mouth, aunty doubted on me and asked if we knew each other.

Alia revealed to aunty about our good friendship and the next few things she said were unbearable for me. She said, "Adarsh always helped me as a friend. Now, he would keep helping me as a brother."

My heart beats lower downed to 40s, and my heart got an ache, and my kidneys got a stroke, whereas my brain was factory reset. These all happened by realising the meaning of the statement stated by Alia.

Aunty gave me a thunderbolt by letting me know that Alia was her daughter. That meant for me that, aunty was my mother in law. (unconventional thought) Showing the hand was the only option that was left for me, and Alia tied me rakhi. My internal soul was stopping me hard not to show the hand. There was a feeling like a dramatic scene was happening with me, and a feeling of suspense music was being played around me by the director of a typical Indian drama series. I imagined as if my face was zoomed thousand times, as seen in typical Indian serials. While bringing my hand forward to her, my hand collapsed. My hand was shivering all the way to home as I didn't want to remember that what actually happened with me in that last hour.

As I was on my way home, I saw the same the stray dogs who were found lying on the streets whom I saw while going to House Number-99. I felt that the dogs gave me a curse on underestimating their life. Then I realised how lucky the dogs were, that they don't have any conditions on living while we the Human Beings have so many conditions, ethics and cultures to be followed. The House Number-99 made me realise that the house proved to be unlucky. It was perfectly relatable that how I felt after my secret crush tied me Rakhi was completely the same feeling that a batsman feels while he or she gets out in the score of 90s and especially in 99, in the game of cricket.

I reduced to meet Alia after that day and distanced myself slowly from her. I made the secret crush remain secret as if never anything happened. There was a possibility that even after getting tied with a Rakhi, we were not officially brothers and sisters by blood, and there was a probability of extending our relationship, but I managed to keep my self-respect and moved on. Even today, I laugh on remembering that day and wandering that what actually happened with me was a comedy or a tragedy.

Fake Smile

I have a fake smile;

I use it as a missile.

To hide struggles and problems;

But not to win politics.

Smiles may be fake;

Expressions may be fake.

But intentions are one;

Never hurt anyone.

Massive success is the best revenge;

So why to be an average.

Play the game of Life;

To win fame and positive vibe.

You are the one who will do it;

Because others are not capable of it.

You will get what you deserve;

Unlike the Government reserve.

CHAPTER SEVEN

Uncovering Thoughts

Coming all the way to my 24 years of my life, I have realised and discovered some of the unconventional thoughts and some of my own created principles that can relatable. Life is not as critical as it looks, but we human beings make it look critical.

A man has unlimited potential within him or her. He or she can perform multiple tasks, at the same time and achieve numerous things at the same age. In this generation, people focus on merry-making and give parties more priority. Yes, it is a very good practice to communicate and become friends with unknown strangers. But that shoots well if they are able to earn their own bread and butter. People put stickers on their automobiles that- "Dad Gifted", letting all the passersby know that their automobile is being gifted by their father. But the best feeling would come if they put stickers as "Self-Owned".

In the meanwhile, after searching for some job vacancy for my father, on surfing the internet and searching through agencies, all of our family members failed miserably. There was a negative vibe surrounded all surrounded around the house. Finally, my father revealed that he had a plan-B with him. He decided to run a business through a partnership with one of his old friends, who was also removed from the job for the same reason. So, finally, after five months of unemployment, he started to manage the business with his business partner. Contribution of capital was the only problem at the beginning, which was solved through the savings and some from the help of the family relatives.

Students in this era are developing a new practice of dominating over their teacher and taunting them when they get any golden chance. They pretend to be mature enough at a very young age, which is no doubt a very good sign of development of practices. But where the maturity goes when the very same children who were taunting the same teacher, start throwing pieces of chalks on each other like kids and complain fake complaints to the teachers like the kids to whom they were taunting minutes ago. So that proves to be very much ironical, isn't it?

This is a type of era where we find twelve to thirteen years old student couples having a night out, whereas a twenty-five-year-old guy is not able to get a girl. The mindset of students has been drastically evolved, from where teachers used to change seats of the students and used to make one boy one girl seat arrangement which was marked as punishment has now turned heaven for the students.

So, I have also observed that most of us are very afraid of going outside all alone without any friends or without even parents to any nearby shop or even eating in a vendor's shop all alone. I had also faced that often times when initially, I used to go to the nearby food stall to bring some sort of food or even to any grocery shop to purchase any sort of items. I discovered that it not only happens with the kids, but it also happens to many teenagers as well as adults. The only reason I found behind it was that we are not afraid to face the person present in the vendor's shop, but we are afraid of something that is present in the wallet or in the pocket or in a purse. Yes, that's the money we are afraid of. For example, when we are eating in a vendor's shop, we often wonder that what if the money that was present in the wallet while coming from home, would have fallen somewhere on the road. Then while paying to the shopkeeper, what would be our reaction and what would we do in such a situation, if we would have lost our wallet somewhere on the road and we are also all alone to handle the situation. It is very much scary to think such situation if we are staying in a five-star hotel and at the time of check out, we would have lost our debit or credit card as well as the money in the wallet.

This is just an unconventional thought that most of us wander, and that's the sole reason I found, behind many teenagers scared to face an unknown shopkeeper when he or she is all alone. We keep on thinking such thoughts while eating in a street vendor's shop and miss the taste of the food that we are eating.

Everything we dream of life and all the wishes we do to get in our life is already there with us. We often dream of having a supercar standing under our garage. The stunning looks of the supercar would give a sense of satisfaction that can be easily imagined, but in reality, we think that it is almost next to impossible. But I think that we can achieve and get anything that we want. We can get the most expensive supercar, or own the most expensive house or anything that we want. But for that, hard work is mostly expected from us, which is the most common phrase that we hear. But, according to me, everything is already prepared for us, but we have to reach there to bring it. For example, in a hotel, the food that we need is already prepared for us. That's how success is. We need to reach the hotel from our home in order to get the food that we need, unlike the online food delivery system, where food comes to you. I can indicate that the online food delivery system is for the people who are already successful or not in their zero levels, where success comes to them. But while we are going to a hotel, we are travelling some sort of distance, and I will indicate that that is the hard work and the destination, the hotel is the success. Life is very easy to understand if we start observing things.

I had gone through three girls at the twenty-two years of my youth life, which gave me the right lessons from each of them. Velina, Parul and Alia contributed their role in my life and taught me that love is not complicated, but the right love has a different spark from others.

Velina was the one who was the most decent girl. She gave a message that love is to be done at the right age. There is a lot of difference between love and attraction. One should be matured enough to handle responsibilities. Whereas, Parul gave me a lesson that love is blind. We do a lot of nonsense things that degrade our impression. We should have a good self-consciousness that what we are doing at a certain time is right or wrong. And finally, in the case of Alia, I haven't realised till date that what actually happened to me was a comedy or a tragedy (Laughs). But the best lesson that I got from Alia was that never do something that is going to degrade in one's self-respect.

Finally, after three months of starting the business, I was happy to see the old shine on my parent's face that was missing for the last five months. Everything started to be good again, and it was again perfectly proved that struggling and bad days never remain forever. It would end, on some random day but we have to keep going and should never stick on one place as well as never give up.

Hit It Hard

You are a batsman on crease;
Play on the field but don't freeze.
If you have no idea of the ball.'
Surely, your stumps will fall.

Attack each ball, seeing the opportunity;
Either you will get out or get a boundary.
Think positive and be positive;
Because there is no way of being negative.

Think life as a batsman on the field;
Hit every ball to the top of the hill.
Think every ball as an opportunity;
Never give up against the majority.

Missed a ball? Hit the next;

Attempt every time to your best.

You are here to win the game,

Finally, earn all your fame.

www.ingramcontent.com/pod-product-compliance
Lightning Source LLC
Chambersburg PA
CBHW022201160726
48282CB00024B/284
9788193843680